ABOUT THE AU

From Homes Under the Hammer and Bargain Hunt, to Killing Eve and the Fast and Furious franchise, Mark Clementson has worked in the Film and TV industry for more than twenty years, these days with the Locations department.

As a Wordsmith, Hellenophile and Creative, Mark also writes for Travel.gr, is published in The Archangel and the White Hart anthology, and was winner of the Reader's Digest short story competition in 2015. He has written two short films which have been made by River Crossing Productions – The Lift (2016) and The Glove (2018).

Mark holds an MA in Creative Writing from the University of London (Birkbeck), is a member of Directors UK, and of Verulam Writers.

The Further Adventures of Clement Golightly is Mark's first short story collection. There are two novels and another short story collection on the way.

Mark's debut feature, MODERN, is due to shoot in October 2024.

He lives 20 miles from the centre of London with his wife, two children, two cats, and a dog.

THE FURTHER ADVENTURES OF CLEMENT GOLIGHTLY

by Mark Clementson

COPYRIGHT NOTICE

A Singular Book

First published in 2022

No part of this book may be used or reproduced in any manner whatsoever without written permission, except in the case of brief quotations embodied in critical articles and reviews.

Copyright © 2022 Mark Clementson

All rights reserved.

ISBN: 9798367080001

For T

For Z

For H

No-one is perfect

You come pretty close

CONTENTS

1	Against the Odds	1
2	Glass Desk	5
3	Travel Broadens the Mind	15
4	Ceremony	16
5	Guide You Home	18
6	The World Outside	21
7	Colin	25
8	Court in a Trap	38
9	One Wednesday	39
10	Leaving	43
11	Trench Warfare	46
12	Something Had to be Done	51
13	The Pips on Radio 4	53
14	Past, Present, and Future	59
15	Secure in the Knowledge that Everything Happens for a Reason	66
16	The Trouble with Mr. Gibson	70
17	Morning Has Not Yet Broken	75

AGAINST THE ODDS

Five pounds and twenty-seven pence. That's all there was. So I put it all on a horse called 'Fortune Favours the Brave'.

I've never been much of a gambler. Not like Macky. That's why he, of all people, understood what it meant when the doctors told him *his* odds. That was eight months ago and he'd lived all that time with courage like I've never seen.

It was the morning of Macky's funeral. The service was in the afternoon of course; Macky was never a fan of mornings. With the whole day booked off work, I found myself looking at the BestBet website.

Fifty-to-one. Better than the odds they gave Macky. All five pounds and twenty-seven pence in the Bestbet account went on the horse. Trouble was, the race was at ten past two, just as I would be sitting in the church listening to hymns and staring at a wooden box with my old mate's body inside.

The church was full to bursting when they brought Macky in. I was pleased about that. I sat at the back, not with the others. I think they thought I was too upset to be at the front, Macky being my best buddy and all. But I'd found a seat where I could sit against the wall and hide the earpiece in my left ear - the earpiece which led to the tranny radio in my pocket. Macky would have approved.

They brought the coffin in. The congregation stood. I have to confess, I was feeling pretty emotional. I thought my knees were going to give way. Then we sang:

Here am I, Lord. Is it I, Lord?
I have heard you calling in the night.

As we sat down, the race was about to begin.

'Fortune Favours the Brave' looks steady
but he's everything to prove at this level.
Just getting round in touch of the leaders
would be an achievement.

We sat.
The vicar talked.

We're here to remember a friend, colleague,
brother and son, David McLeary.
Our thoughts must be in particular with his mother, Barbara,
his sisters, and...

Macky would have been bored to tears, waiting for the moment he could get to the buffet and the free bar. But he'd have been much happier with a horse-race going on in his ear.

'Letsbee Avenue' just behind 'Cut Your Teeth' and 'Smooth Rider',
with a tight-packed group four lengths back.
These three look like they're going to pull away.

He wouldn't have put his money on a fifty-to-one though.

The vicar was still yabbering on about this bloke he'd never met, checking his notes, making sure he got names and places right. The commentator was building to a climax.

> *'Smooth Rider' has done all his running.*
> *'Groundhog Day' and 'Fortune Favours the Brave'*
> *have joined the front-runners.*
> *With three to go, it's 'Cut Your Teeth', 'Smooth Rider',*
> *'Groundhog Day', and 'Fortune Favours the Brave'.*

I don't know whether it was because of the two worlds colliding, but I noticed for the first time the vicar's long face and prominent equine teeth.

> *And David will be remembered too by the regulars*
> *at the Devonshire Arms.*

The vicar was reaching a climax. He'd done quite well not overdoing the God stuff. I think he could smell heathens and thought it best to get it in under the radar. The commentator was struggling, the end of the race too close to call.

> *'Cut Your Teeth' and 'Fortune Favours the Brave'*
> *are neck and neck.*
> *'Cut your Teeth' has the inside track.*

We were standing again ready for another hymn.

> *'Fortune Favours the Brave' is keeping pace.*
> *Nothing between them.*
> *It's 'Fortune Favours the Brave' and 'Cut Your Teeth'.*

We sang.

> *I see the stars, I hear the rolling thunder,*

Thy power throughout the universe displayed.

The two horses pounded towards the finish line. The congregation sang to the coffin which stayed quiet and still.

Then sings my soul, My Saviour God, to Thee,
How great Thou art, How great Thou art.

And as the hymn echoed around the church, barely anyone heard the man at the back screaming.

Go Macky, You fucking beauty!

GLASS DESK

As the empty columns lay on the screen before him, Charles was scratching a picture of a boat into his desk with his keys. Somewhere in the distance he could hear his name being called.

'Charles.'

But Charles was dreaming of the sea. He was a pirate standing on the bow of a wooden ship. Susan was beside him, her red hair in tight curls falling across her breasts pushed up by her buxom pirate-lady bodice. As the ship rose and sank, it plunged through the ocean, and sea-spray blew against his face.

'Charles!'

The sea disappeared. Susan and her buxom breasts disappeared. He looked up from his desk to see Hawkins standing over him.

'Can I see you in my office Charles?'

Charles had set aside the morning to work on the pensions list for a large bank. The company had promised its employees a carefree retirement to look forward to. They wanted him to crunch the numbers and deliver the good news to their staff. In reality, he knew they would have been better off sticking a fiver under the mattress each week, or betting on the greyhound that takes a shit just before the start of the race.

He was now a senior advisor, which meant three things: A tiny rise in salary, a hugely increased workload, and a much more miserable day-to-day existence. He had a corner desk in an open-plan office, right by the window. On the desk was his computer, a stack of red files containing lists of names and numbers, and a photograph of Susan in a pound-shop frame, his favourite picture of her, taken on a canal boat at the festival two summers ago.

He could see everyone who worked at Carter and Simms: Fiona the PA, freckle-faced and feeble, so meek she might have had a heart attack if anyone had said the word 'knickers'. Justin, the accounts manager, sitting alongside the window in front of him, wearing short-sleeved shirts throughout the winter to show off his toned biceps. Then there was Jason, fat and forty-something, first in, last to leave, desperate to please, desperate for a promotion like the one Charles had received. And lastly, at the end of the room, in his own office, was Hawkins, the boss, handsome and a complete cunt.

Charles followed Hawkins to his office then loitered in the doorway until the boss sat down and waved him in.

It would have been impossible to etch graffiti into Hawkins' glass desk, unless you used a diamond. Like the man himself, everything on the desk was clean, functional, and utterly lifeless: A pot of identical pens, a ruler placed perfectly parallel to the desk's edge, and an unreasonably shiny laptop.

Hawkins sat upright in his chair, looking across the desk at Charles. The expression beneath his neatly parted hair was impossible to read. There was no anger, certainly no warmth, not even any visible signs of curiosity.

'I've noticed you've missed your last four performance targets,' Hawkins slid a piece of paper across the glass surface. 'It seems April was a particularly bad month. I wonder whether...'

Charles was dreaming again. He was back at school, but things were different. He was surrounded by the children in his form at St Swithen's just as he remembered them. But Susan was there too, much younger and wearing his old school uniform. She was standing at the centre of the group of teenagers. They were all looking at him, smiling.

'Charles?'

The young Susan was leaning in toward him, eyeing him dreamily.

'Charles?'

Reluctantly, he returned to the room.

'Look Charles, I like you, I really do, but this…'

'Whatever.'

It was the first thing Charles had said all day, the first thing that had come to mind.

'I'm sorry.' Hawkins was standing now, looking down at him.

'You know,' said Charles, 'Whatever. Don't lose your rag.'

Charles picked up the ruler from the desk.

'Charles. Stop slouching,' said Hawkins, 'I'm sorry to have to say this but I'm extremely concerned about…'

Hawkins was interrupted by the sound of twanging as Charles lay the ruler over the edge of the desk and plucked it with his forefinger. He plucked it again and again, moving the ruler back and forth to change the pitch of the sound.

'Charles, please don't do that.'

Charles plucked a couple more times, then he picked up the sheet of paper containing the statistics of his latest failures, the missed performance targets. He took a quick look at it, and then at Hawkins, before he scrunched the paper into a ball.

'Really Charles, I'm not sure that…'

The paper flew off the end of the ruler and struck Hawkins on the end of the nose. Charles stood.

'I'm sorry,' he said, 'But I've decided this reality shit

is not for me.'

He opened the door and walked out. As he passed through the open-plan office and the faces of Fiona and Justin and Jason looked up at him, he slipped an arm under his shirt and into his armpit. He pumped his arm up and down making a delightful farty sound.

He took the tube to Green Park, to the office where Susan worked. She would be proud of him. They'd talked about what they would do if they didn't have to work all the time, if they were free. And now, he'd done it. 'You need to take control,' she'd said 'Don't let people walk all over you.'

She could quit her job too. They could go away to Italy or Spain, or Australia even. Nothing stood in their way now.

The familiar clatter of the underground train was soothing. He stood at the end of the carriage in the space by the open window. The draft blew around his head, through his hair, in and out of his ears, and he drifted away again.

They were in Italy, outside a little coffee shop. Susan was sitting opposite him at a table laid out with a single flower in a vase, two tiny cups of coffee, and a jug of iced water. For some reason she seemed to have taken up smoking. She was wearing sunglasses and her hair was up in a scarf. Behind her was the Colosseum and a group of Japanese tourists taking pictures.

'I think we should take the train to Venice,' she said letting out a plume of smoke, 'I hear it's lovely at this time of year.'

'The next station is Green Park. Change here for the Jubilee and Piccadilly Lines.'

Her office was only a two-minute walk from the

station. He sprinted up the escalator, out through the ticket barriers, and didn't stop running until he was in the lift on his way up to the seventh floor. In the lift, the dream returned.

They were drinking red wine, sitting at a table in a first-class train carriage. Susan's cigarette was in a holder this time. Her sunglasses were on top of her head. She was wearing a silver ballgown which complimented her stunning grey-blue eyes. The dress was having much the same effect on her breasts as the pirate bodice had.

She blew a smoke-ring.

'I think we should get married in Venice,' she said, 'What do you think?"

'Yes, great,' he said.

She leaned in and kissed him. She tasted of tobacco and wine.

'Seventh floor.'

He walked straight past the receptionist, through the office and past Susan's colleagues tapping away at their computers, towards her desk at the back.

She was wearing her hair in a ponytail, which he didn't like. And she was wearing a blouse buttoned high up the neck. Soon he would take her away from this all this, from the restrictions of this place. She was going to be so happy, so proud of him.

'Charles?' She said, 'You look dreadful. What's happened?'

Did he look dreadful? He felt great.

'I'm free Susan. I've left my job.'

'Oh Charles.'

'So I've come to get you.'

'Me?'

'Yes. I thought maybe Italy first. And then whatever

takes your fancy.'

'Have you gone completely mad?'

'We've talked about it so much. Now I'm free. Just tell them you're leaving. It's finally happening.'

But she wasn't moving. Why wasn't she getting up from her desk? And why was everyone staring at him? He could hear voices muttering around the room.

'I have work to do,' she said, 'I think you should go home.'

'Probably right,' he said, 'You get things sorted here, and I'll see you later.'

'Oh Charles, that's not what I mean. I'm sorry if...'

'You don't need to worry about a thing,' he said.

She wasn't as strong as him. The thought of leaving behind all this conformity, this reality. Of course, it was going to be difficult for her.

She finally stood up. Everyone was watching. A woman came over to her desk.

'Susan, do you need some help?'

She waved them away.

'Charles. Go home. On your own. And call your work and see if it's not too late to get your job back.'

This wasn't how it was supposed to work. She loved him. They were going to be together. This office, this life, it wasn't good enough for her, for them.

'Why are you saying that?' he said.

She sat down and looked at her computer screen.

He felt a hand on his arm. He looked round to see a man in a suit and tie smiling at him and pulling him towards the exit.

'Susan,' he called.

Why had he tried to talk with her in front of all those people? Of course she'd been frightened. Just like he had been for all these years. It was difficult for others to understand, he knew that. Look at Hawkins. Pensions administration was as good as it got for the likes of him. But not for Charles. And not for Susan. She wanted to be with him. And he needed to be with her. Together they would soon leave everything and everyone else behind.

Back at home, he needed to keep busy. He washed the dishes from breakfast, then hoovered and dusted the whole house. He tidied everything away, leaving surfaces clear of clutter, cupboards and drawers neatly organised. He re-arranged the collection of carrier bags under the sink. He decluttered the cutlery draw. He even sorted through the drawer of lost things for items with no specific place or purpose - screws and bolts and nails, keys from long-forgotten locks, and the pair of handcuffs he'd found behind the wardrobe when he'd moved into the flat.

And then he was tired. Really tired. He brushed his teeth and, without getting out of his clothes, he went to bed where he dreamed of Susan.

They were in an open-topped car driving through the Alps. Matt Monro provided the soundtrack. She was smiling and shielding her eyes from the sun. Several strands of hair had escaped her headscarf and were blowing back and forth across her face. He pulled over at the side of the road where there was a sheer drop down to the valley floor. He put his arms around her. He breathed in the smell of the countryside and the scent of her. She kissed him and then took a cigarette from a silver case. He took a gold lighter from his jacket pocket and held out a flame for her.

'I've never been so happy,' she said, 'Let's keep driving forever.'

But then she was enveloped by the smoke and everything changed. They weren't in the Alps anymore. They were in a London pub and she was standing beside him as he sat at the bar. Her hair was long and straight. She was wearing a leather jacket and trousers.

She took a long drag on the cigarette she was smoking and then stubbed it out in the ashtray.

'It's over,' she said, 'I never loved you.'

'But Susan.'

'Who could love you? You're a fool.'

'I want to look after you,' he said.

'You can't even look after yourself.'

He woke, more tired than when he had gone to bed. It was quarter to four in the morning. But at least he had a plan.

He knew the train times by heart. He'd commuted for long enough. And he often went out walking in the mornings when he couldn't sleep - which was when he'd first met Susan walking her dog in the early hours. So he knew that the first train was at exactly twenty past five. And, being the first train of the day, it was always on time.

What was the name of her dog? He simply couldn't remember. Bradley? Brockley? It didn't matter anyhow. The dog would have to find a new home now that Susan was going away.

He never thought he would have a use for the handcuffs. But he took them from the drawer, tested them out by attaching them to the radiator in the hall, and then he put them, along with the tiny key, into his coat pocket.

He made a flask of tea, making sure he left the kitchen clean and tidy, and then he put on a jumper. The sun wasn't yet up and it would be cold outside. He made sure he secured all three locks on the front door. It wasn't a bad neighbourhood, but most thieves were opportunists and if they saw he was out then he was asking for trouble.

As he walked to the park, for some reason, he

thought of his mother. He was at primary school, sitting on the carpet playing with building blocks while she talked to the teacher.

'Such a quiet child,' said the teacher.

'I know. Sometimes it's like he's hardly there at all,' said his mother.

Charles was building a tower, then a house, then an entire town.

'He never plays with the others,' the teacher said.

'No. He likes to build imaginary worlds with his toys. And he writes these long stories,' said his mother lowering her voice to a whisper, 'But I've never read one. He doesn't like me to see them.'

'A loner,' said the teacher, 'That's how I'd describe him.'

It wasn't something Charles would have chosen to be. He would much rather have been an eagle, soaring high over the world, or perhaps a honey badger like the one he'd seen on the Discovery Channel. Honey badgers were wily and aggressive. They took control of a Situation. They knew how to survive. That's how Charles wanted to be.

He headed across the football pitches and past the small cafe where he often sat and waited for her. He snuck through the hedge at the back of the tennis courts, down the bank, and was soon standing by the train track. He put down his flask next to the rails and removed the handcuffs and his mobile phone from his pocket. The track ran right alongside the park where Susan and her dog came walking each morning. And the park was just a few hundred yards from where she lived.

He lay down on the tracks and attached the handcuffs to one of his wrists. Then he attached the other end to one of the rails. He made himself as comfortable as he could while he tapped a message on his phone to Susan:

Urgent.
If you love me meet me at the back of the tennis courts in Chester Park by five fifteen.
I'll be waiting. I love you.

He checked that the message had been sent and then put down the phone. He sat up as best he could with his wrist attached to the rail and poured himself a cup of tea. The birds were singing. There was no sound of the morning's traffic yet. It was still dark but behind the large oak tree on the other side of the tracks he could see a patch of light where the sun was beginning to rise. He sipped the tea and looked down at his phone. It was four forty-seven. Susan would be here soon.

He took the tiny key from his pocket and threw it onto the bank where he could see it but could no longer reach it. Then he took his phone and threw that too. He lay down across the train tracks. He felt good, but he was still very tired. He could hear his heart beating. It was a beautiful morning. He closed his eyes and began to dream.

He was sitting on the carpet again in his primary school classroom. He'd made a house using several dozen wooden blocks. His mother and the teacher were gone now. There was a little red-haired girl sitting cross-legged on the carpet next to him.

'Can I help?' she said. She didn't smile. She just blinked, twice. And he noticed her grey-blue eyes.

Charles handed her a block. She looked carefully at the structure on the carpet. Then the red-haired girl blinked once more and reached out and carefully placed the block on top of the house.

TRAVEL BROADENS THE MIND

Having invented a time machine, and tested it by sending Charles the hamster one minute into the future, Henry wondered where to go first.
After much thought and a bacon sandwich, he decided two thousand years forward would be interesting.

Whir. Whizz. Coloured spirals.

Things look different. The buildings are gone. There is only grass and trees and flowers.
And a pig, wearing dark glasses.
Knowing nothing of the 41st century, Henry approaches.
The pig stands on two legs, holds up a laser-rod, and shoots Henry between the eyes.
His family will eat well. Humans are scarce in these parts.

CEREMONY

It was a dark and stormy night. And there's me, in my pants, looking out at the garden.

You would've laughed yourself silly.
It was exactly a year, as you requested, a year to the day. I know you think of me as forgetful. But I remembered it all, every word you said.
I laid out your clothes: the blue top, the mini-skirt and leggings, even the boots, just like you said. And next to them mine: the shirt you said wouldn't have looked out of place in a circus and the jeans which were inappropriate for a first date. I'd worn them as I walked to the garden carrying your clothing. I tried not to blub pathetically as I thought about how I'd carried you inside the first time we came here.
I placed the drinks between the two piles of clothes as planned, a glass of white wine for you, a pint of Guinness for me. I hope you don't mind, but I took a sip from each.
We never talked about how best to set everything on fire. As this was to be the last time I followed one of your stupid plans, I thought I should do things properly - as it turned out, a little excessively. But I didn't want our life together to be marked by a puff of smoke. I covered the clothes with paraffin, then the lawn. And I may have spilt just a little on the garden fence.
I was crying, pretty heavily by this point, could hardly have been expected to be thinking clearly. As you suspected, even after a year I was reluctant to let you go. But I conducted your ceremony, just as you said, marked

the occasion, said goodbye to you forever. Time to move on. And I will.

But your idea brought more of a certain end to things than you could've imagined.

At first, as a waft of flame engulfed our clothes, I thought how proud you would be. I'd made it through, done things just as we planned. But then it sort of quickly got out of hand. I couldn't put the fire out before it reached the fence. I blew on it, hit it with the back of a spade. Nothing.

Having reached the fence, it licked the branches of the apple tree which were dangling near the washing line next door. I looked up to see Mr Johnson's face, peering out from his bedroom window at me in my pants, illuminated by the flames now spread to a row of his own underwear.

I dashed into the house, fetched a saucepan of water and threw it on the lawn. You won't be surprised to hear it didn't have much effect.

I'm afraid when the firemen arrived I was kneeling amidst the charred remains of our clothing, as our garden, and the Johnson's, raged with flames. And I was laughing. Apparently, I was looking up at the sky rambling about the circumference of the moon.

Let me reassure you though, the house is fine. But I shan't be going back. You are no longer there.

I'm staying with Mum, just for a while. There's a flat for rent down by the canal. I think I'll get rid of the car, go for more walks like you always said I should. Maybe even cycle to work along the towpath.

Thank you. You clever, mischievous, and beautiful woman. This was the most awful thing I have ever done. But you were right, a year is long enough to be sad.

GUIDE YOU HOME

There's no black people in our village. Can't imagine why any black person would want to be the first, neither.

Dad says they're lazy. 'Wouldn't get no darky working down't pit.'

I think about Mam's diamond engagement ring. And I want to ask him where he thinks the gold and the diamond came from. Not his fucking coal mine, that's for sure.

The man sings in half-English. I can understand most of the words, but not always what they mean. Which is weird. Cause I like that I can't really get what he's saying. He's always smiling. He closes his eyes and he makes that chok-ee-chok sound with his guitar.

I think back to when I first saw him a year ago, when I first sat on this kerb. I know it's exactly a year cause the Christmas lights have just gone up and it's bastard cold, just like it were then.

But he still sings. Every time I come here.

It costs me nought to get here. So I can spend me dinner money on some toast and a cup of tea and have twenty pee left to put in the man's hat.

There's this one song I like, 'bout a big tree. And the man says about chopping it down with a small axe.

Me Dad always calls me the runt of the litter, but I reckon I can be a small axe. And he's one big bastard of a tree.

I've never spoken to the man before. He always winks at me when I arrive and sit down on the kerb. Then he sings some more and I drink my tea. But today he stops playing and puts down his guitar. He walks over and sits down next to me. He smiles and bumps his shoulder against mine. He smells of tobacco and liquorice.

He doesn't say anything for a long time. I think about whether I should run away. Then he says:

'How old are you, lad?'

And he doesn't speak funny. He speaks like one of me Dad's mates, even though he doesn't look like them.

'Fifteen,' I say, not looking at him.

'Not very tall,' he says, pulling a packet of fags from his pocket.

This makes me cry. Which I hate. And I want to run away. I'm not scared of the man, but I am embarrassed as fuck.

He offers me a cigarette. I sniff and I take one, even though I've only ever taken a couple of drags before. And it stunts your growth and I'm already the runt of the litter.

We light our cigarettes with a match. I manage not to cough. But I feel sick and I must look stupid. I don't even look anywhere near fourteen, let alone fifteen. And I'm sitting on the kerb in a strange city with a black man and smoking cigarettes.

The tears have gone. And I imagine me Dad seeing me, which makes me laugh.

'What's so funny?' says the man.

I don't answer. I stub the fag out on the floor.

'I like your music,' I say. Me voice sounds funny. Me throat feels sore.

'Thanks,' says the man. He gets to his feet, 'Need to play. Got to earn some money. You staying?'

I want to stay. But I'm cold. And I'll be in trouble if I'm not home when school turns out. And the train ride takes nearly an hour.

'Stay for one last tune,' he says. He picks up his guitar, strums it to check it's alive, 'It's just for you, this one. My number one fan."

'What's it called?' I ask.

'Jah will guide you home.' he says.

He starts playing. The strumming is bouncy and he taps his left foot. Then he's singing in that strange language not at all like the man sitting on the kerb.

I can't hear all the words, but it's a happy tune with some sadness in it, like all his other tunes.

When he stops, I get up from the kerb and go over and put twenty pee in his hat. He bends down, picks it up and gives it back to me. He wraps it in me fist, holds on to me hand and looks into me eyes.

'Buy yourself another tea,' he says.

I don't know who Jar is or even where home is anymore.

'See you tomorrow,' I say.

'Safe journey,' says the man.

THE WORLD OUTSIDE

It was time for Emma's break. She took one last look through the open door at the couple laughing in room fourteen, and went off in search of coffee. Despite having been a nurse for ten years, she was no closer to understanding how people coped, holding on to the good things that life has to offer, until the very end.

Emma sat with her coffee and looked out at the street. The wind seemed crazy today. People passed by holding onto their coats, struggling along, pushing against the wind. Newspapers and crisp packets flew around their feet.

Inside the hospital Emma was safe and warm. But she wasn't happy. What had she done in her life so far? Watching the world outside she yearned for the courage to go out and grab life. She thought again about the couple. What had brought them such happiness?

Richard was fucked. And he knew it.

The Raymond account had been his last hope. Fifty thousand would have paid the suppliers allowing him to concentrate on the next big client.

He took a swig from the whisky bottle and surveyed the room. The furniture would soon be gone; he'd already packed much of the paperwork into boxes. He'd put this business before everything else. He'd neglected his parents, his friends, and the woman he loved.

And then there was Marian. She had fought to the last to make it work.

Now he couldn't even afford to pay Marian's wages. He would have to tell her immediately.

Marian was finished. And no-one seemed to care.

Just five years from retirement she had no chance of

finding another job. She knew the company was struggling. But there had always been hope. Finally, the moment had come. She'd cleared her desk and left Richard and his whisky alone in the office. She thought of all the effort she'd made over the last six years and wondered what she would do now.

Now she couldn't afford to make the trip.

She would have to tell Stella today.

Stella was hopeful. Her mother had taken some convincing.

So what if she'd lost her job? Stella knew this was an opportunity to finally visit her and Mike, and the grandchildren she hadn't seen for five years. More than that, it was time to sell the house and come and live with them in Toronto. Stella had a wonderful husband and two beautiful children. To have her mother close by would make everything perfect.

Now she just needed to persuade Mike to let her mother come and stay.

She would talk to him today.

Mike was sweating. And the world outside ceased to exist.

He lay on his back, his hands cupped under Grace's buttocks as they rose up and came down. He was feverish. And then it was over. It was just seconds before he began to think of Stella. She'd given up everything for him, coming to Canada because he wanted to. He loved her with all his heart. So, what was he doing here?

Now he must put an end to the affair.

He would tell Grace today.

Grace was silent. And Mike had fallen asleep.

She lay naked, beads of sweat turning cold upon her chest. She stared up at the ceiling and wondered why she kept doing this. Ellie said there was something wrong with people who fucked blokes old enough to be their father, but she ached to be with him all the time.

Now she had decided.

She would demand that he leave his wife today.

Ellie was planning.

And she was loving every minute of it.

The seating plan was almost done. But Grace was a problem. She'd insisted that she'd be bringing a partner. But this man of hers had a wife and children. You don't give those things up lightly. And she expected him to fly all the way to London with her to attend the wedding? Ellie couldn't think about her best friend anymore. She loved her and worried for her in equal measure. Her thoughts turned to Carl. Would he live to see her get married?

Now she was wondering.

She must visit the hospital today.

Carl was laughing. And it hurt.

But he wouldn't show her his pain. They had always shared a sense of humour, him and Michelle. And because of this he loved her. They would have had beautiful children – if she had chosen him. But he knew long before the cancer that she wanted Richard.

Now time had run out.

He would let her go today.

Michelle was watching. And Carl drifted off to sleep.

Soon Carl would be gone and she wouldn't need to break his heart. She loved him passionately, but she was never 'in' love with him. Not like she was with Richard:

Richard the workaholic, Richard the borderline alcoholic, Richard who she couldn't bear to live without.

Now she knew.

She would be with Richard today.

Richard was thinking. And his thoughts travelled in circles.

The whisky hadn't helped. He thought of Michelle. As he poured another glass, he was ashamed. The company was gone. Marian had left in tears. And then there was Carl, his best friend in the world, lying in a hospital bed. He hadn't visited in weeks.

Now he knew.

He would go to see Carl tomorrow.

As Emma watched through the window, the wind seemed to calm suddenly. She noticed the trees outside, lining the otherwise grey city street. It was Spring and blossom was beginning to appear; the whites, pinks and yellows which brought smiles to people's faces as winter left.

She glanced at her fob-watch. Her allotted fifteen minutes was over. As she headed back along the corridor, she saw the Doctor rush through the door of room fourteen. She caught the eye of the young woman standing outside just as she burst into tears. Emma reached out and held the woman's arm. She knew that sometimes people look to a stranger for support.

COLIN

I first met him on Hampstead Heath. We were sitting up a tree smoking a joint. There was the usual crowd, Jim and Gavin, Sal and me. And then there was Colin, ponsing fags, telling some seedy tale about a girl he'd copped off with the night before, and then talking up his job in sales.

I don't know who'd invited him.

'Best figures of the month, again,' he said, 'I'm looking at three grand commission.' He sucked hard on the spliff and neglected to pass it around. And I got my first look at that smug expression, that stupid big nose spreading as he smiled.

'Enough money to pay for a decent holiday,' he continued, 'America maybe. I've always wanted to do route 66.'

'Sweet,' said Sal.

'Thing about sales is, you've got to get to know your prey, get to their weakness as quick as possible. Some people part with their money out of fear, some like to be flattered, others, they want to be full-on chatted up like some premium-rate phone line. It's prostitution really. I put out, and they hand over the cash.'

'You must get some people who just tell you to fuck off?' It was the first time Sal had met him too.

'You can't think like that,' he said. He sat up and looked over at her. She shouldn't have spoken to him, shouldn't have encouraged his boring conversation. 'I can take money from anyone.'

'Isn't that a bit immoral?' she asked.

'Morals are for weaklings and God-botherers,' he said. And he actually fucking winked at her.

Even Colin's mother had given up on him, fucked off to live in the south of France with some bloke she'd met at her art classes or something. I heard the story from Gavin who'd heard it from Jim who'd heard it from a bloke in the pub. She left her son in his childhood home, mortgage-free, told him she wouldn't be coming back and not to forget to feed the cat.

I never saw him buy a drink or roll a joint. And I never experienced him shutting the fuck up and letting someone else choose the topic of conversation. Take that time at Jim and Gavin's flat. I loved it there. We'd had so many good times there, the four of us. It always made me smile, the cushions and throws laid out by Gavin, Jim's books and magazines and pens and mugs littering every surface. They were a perfect match and chalk and cheese too, Jim from East London, Gavin from Fulham in the West. Jim dropping his 'h's and unable to pronounce his 'r's. Gavin, the product of a 'nice' school, spoke properly with a barely-open mouth. They were great fun to watch together, great fun to be with, until Colin came along and got in the way.

No-one knew who'd invited him that night either. But there he was drinking one of the cans of Stella I'd brought round.

'Alloy wheels,' he said, 'Leather interior and heated seats. Got them thrown in for free. Female sales assistant. Can I help it if I'm charming?'

'Isn't it a bit of a waste of money?' said Sal, 'You know, buying a sports car when you live in a city where the traffic tends to travel at five miles an hour?'

'I'll take you for a ride, wherever you want to go,' he said, 'You'll soon change your mind.'

'Sweet,' said Sal.

'Wanker' is what I was thinking.

That was why I admired Sal. Because everything was 'sweet'. Everything in her world was fun and extraordinary and full of endless wonder. 'Sweet', the very best word I could have used to describe Sal herself.

'Been earning more of them big bonuses?' asked Jim.

'Just set up on my own actually, selling ad-space online,' said Colin, 'The car's all part of the image. You've got to look the part. Reckon I'll be turning over close to a mill' a year within eighteen months.'

'Fuck off,' said Jim.

'I guess you do have to be ambitious,' said Gavin.

Colin cracked open another can of beer.

Sal started rolling a spliff, delicately licking the end of a cigarette paper. Sticking three papers together, she made the perfect length five-person joint. She was crumbling hash into the paper laid flat on a David Bowie LP and didn't look up at me as she spoke.

'What about you? Any chance of you making a mill' anytime soon?'

'He doesn't have the drive to make big money,' Colin said, waving his beer can in my general direction, "No offence. I mean, there's nothing wrong in that, working nine to five for someone else, letting all the shit be their problem. I can see the attraction of heading back home to an acceptable wife and a box set.'

I knew I hated him completely by the time my birthday came around. It wasn't a party as such, but it was definitely my birthday, and that was why we were all together in the Coach and Horses. Jim and Gavin were playing darts, spending most of the time laughing at their lack of ability. I was sitting at a table with Sal and Colin.

I was pretty skint and feeling quite low. I wasn't working back then. Dad's shop had just closed down, which had left me out of a job, and I hadn't started looking for anything else, what with it being nearly Christmas. There didn't seem much point. You shouldn't need to buy a round on your birthday anyway. But everyone's glasses were empty, so I got up and offered.

'Same again,' Jim called from over from the dart board.

'Me too,' said Gavin, 'Doesn't matter how much we drink, we're not going to get any worse.'

And they descended into laughter once more.

'We should go on to shots,' said Colin.

'Yeah,' said Sal, 'Line 'em up. There's only an hour til closing.'

So I went to the bar, alone. And I was pissed off. I didn't want to buy Colin a drink. I just wanted to be with the others. Actually, things were worse than that. I wanted nothing more than to take a pint glass, smash it on the edge of the bar, then go back and shove it up his ridiculous nose.

But I didn't.

We were all mightily pissed by the time the bell rung at the bar. We staggered up the hill. Colin was telling Jim and Gavin some story about a friend in the music business.

'I'll see if I can rustle you up a pair of backstage passes.'

They were lapping it up like a pair of fan boys.

Sal was way out in front. I tried to keep up. But she ran ahead. As we got to the brow of the hill, she started pulling off her jacket, intent on going for a swim in the pond. She reached the edge and sat down on the floor kicking off each of her boots in turn. She was singing Silent Night like Marilyn Monroe would have done for JFK. She took her time over the last line 'slee-eep in heeeeeavenly peeeaaace', then she got to her feet and jumped in. She screamed as the cold hit her and she set off on a breast-stroke breaking into a new tune.

'Dashing through the snow…'

The others came running up to where she'd left her jacket and boots, threw off their shirts and shoes, and were soon in the water slapping around like teenagers at the public baths. I climbed in, fully clothed. I'd have looked like a real saddo if I'd been the only one not to go in. It was bloody freezing, colder than it was the day I'd stood with my dad watching that stupid balsa-wood yacht sink when I was nine years old.

Pretty soon they started splashing me. I laughed it off. And I patted a few splashes back at Gavin.

'Tsunami,' Shouted Colin, flopping down on the surface, face first, his arms out wide. Water engulfed me. Everyone laughed.

'That's enough,' said Sal getting out, 'I think I'm sober now.'

Her dress clung to her breasts, her nipples prominent evidence of the cold. I could see Colin watching her right up until the moment she covered herself with her jacket. Then he and Jim and Gavin got out and threw on their shirts. Sal flagged down a cab. She opened the door but before getting in she turned to us.

'Mwah,' she air-kissed, 'Safe journey home you sad bunch of losers.'

The other three were making for the main road.

'Wanna get a cab with us?' asked Colin. I wanted to punch him hard in the face, shatter his fat nose, or maybe push him into the road and watch him get flattened under a bus.

'Nah,' I said.

I walked all the way home. And I woke up the next morning feeling like shit. I was miserable, and twenty-nine years old.

Sal hated him too of course. Although, she was the

very definition of 'nice', and she would never have told him to fuck right off, which is exactly what he needed to hear. I tried talking about it a week later when we were waiting for a bus home at Golders Green station.

'Who the fuck invites him?' I asked.

'Who invites you? Or me?' she said, rummaging in her bag, 'We're just part of the group.'

'Yes, but he isn't is he?'

I wanted her to agree. I wanted her to say how much he got on her tits, all the time. I wanted her to say that the four of us should meet up in the future and make sure he wasn't there. I wanted her to say she hated his fat fucking nose and had a raging desire to rip his face open with shards of newly-shattered pint glass.

She pulled a hairbrush from her bag and ran it through her hair.

'Do you ever think about getting old?' she said.
I didn't really. I liked things how they were.

'Sometimes I think it would be nice to be old,' she said, 'to have already made all your mistakes. Old people have anything to worry about. Apart from death of course.'

'My Nan will be ninety next year,' I said.

'Sweet,' She ran the brush through her hair again. 'Have you applied for any jobs yet?' she asked.

'Not yet,' I said.

The bus arrived. We got on. And I don't remember what we talked about on the journey. I only remember the silences in between.

So that's how it continued. The four of us had become five, with Colin now an ever-present.

I just wanted to talk to Jim and Gavin about music and films. And I wanted to talk to Sal about her latest blog post, or the idiots she worked with, or even what she'd had for dinner last night. But there was Colin, always there, like a splinter wedged beneath a fingernail.

I couldn't find a job in January, or in February. I was pissed off. And the shit we had to put up with from Colin was getting me down. How could I be expected to find work when all I could think of was how my friends, the group I had always relied on, was being destroyed by him. It had all been so perfect, and then into this tranquil lake around which we had been sailing together for so long, came Colin. Every time I looked at that stupid big nose, the nostrils flaring as he spoke, I despised him more. I fantasised about stubbing out my cigarette in his face, watching the shock in his eyes, inhaling the smell of his smoldering nasal hairs.

In March, Sal went away for a fortnight with work, to some sales fair in Berlin. The others were going out on the Friday night just after she'd left. I didn't want to go, but Jim said I was becoming a miserable old bastard. And Gavin agreed. So I decided to go. I didn't want my friends worrying about me.

Colin shouldn't be able to stop me from seeing everyone. I vowed not to talk to him. I could enjoy the conversation with Jim and Gavin like always, and I could just stay calm and chose not to talk with Colin. I mean, why the fuck should I? He wasn't my friend.

We had a table in the corner, the four of us. It felt quite different, being just blokes. And, in all honesty, Colin was less of a wanker. Still a wanker, still a big-nosed bastard who never buys a drink. But for once he didn't dominate the conversation. Jim talked a lot, about some bands he'd been listening too, and books he'd been reading. And Gavin teased him about his love of Georgette Heyer and Charlaine Harris. And I told them about what had happened to the shop, how Dad had finally decided to give up and that he was doing ok but he was sad that it had ended so badly. I told them about my search for a job, and, to tell the truth, I still felt a bit unable to get back out there.

I kept my promise to myself and I didn't talk to Colin at all. I felt much calmer. At least, I did until the bell rang for time at the bar.

Gavin went to get a last round in. Jim went off to the Gents. I looked down at my phone, trying to pass the time before they returned.

'Everything alright mate?' said Colin.

Mate? That one word. It brought back all my violent feelings towards him, all my hatred of his smug face and his self-righteous tone. I wasn't his mate. And he fucking well knew it. He knew we all hated him. He wasn't one of us.

'Just texting Sal,' I replied.

'Say hi from me,' he said, 'Or maybe 'guten tag.'

Fucking smug, smarmy, son-of-a-bitch, cunting bastard twat.

It was a hot summer. There were weekends on the Heath, escaping the heat, drinking whisky straight from the bottle, smoking endlessly. Jim had got a tattoo and taken to wearing sleeveless t-shirts - some old aboriginal lettering formed a band around his upper arm. It looked alright really. But we all took the piss anyway, especially Gavin.

'We were on the tube yesterday next to some Aussie bloke who says it reads "Your mum shags koalas", or something like that.'

'At least she'd smell nice,' said Sal.

'What?' we all asked.

'You know, her fanny would be all eucalyptus fresh.'

I noticed Sal was hardly drinking. She smoked a lot though. She was permanently hamster-eyed and either mellow or a little bit lost. She took to wearing a cute combination of short, strappy summer dresses and DM boots.

'When is this bloody heat going to stop?' said Jim.
'I'm loving it.' said Sal.
'I don't want the summer to end,' I said. Which was true. I was becoming a bit frightened by the future. Mum and Dad were still subbing me, still with the minimum amount of disapproval. I didn't want to get back into the world of work until the Autumn.

Colin was the next to turn the big three-oh. And at the beginning of September, he turned up with these posh invitations to a party at his house.

'I'd love you all to be there,' he said.

I couldn't think of anything worse.

'Gotta mark the occasion,' he said, 'Got lots of work friends who'll be there. Maybe we can find you a job, eh?' He slapped me across the shoulder.

I could imagine his stupid bloody house. Glass porch at the front with his Hunter wellingtons and golf umbrella to one side. Then into the oak-floored hallway past the architectural sketches in frames to the open plan lounge-kitchen-diner to see him sitting there on the Playstation as if it's ok for a grown man to want to pretend to be a special ops soldier on a mission to save civilisation.

I turned away and started talking to Sal. I didn't want to think about Colin and his stupid party and his stupid friends and his stupid fucking house.

The party was a week away and we'd all agreed to go. Like I had any fucking choice at all. The others had been talking about it over beer and chips in the Bull and Bush.

'Looking forward to it mate, seeing you into your old age,' said Jim.

'I do love a good party,' said Gavin, 'Tell me, who's doing the music?'

'A cousin of mine has organised all that for me. But if there's anything in particular you want to hear…'

That's how it went on. I never got to talk to any of them.

When we left the pub the last of the day's light was slipping away. We were all quite drunk, particularly Gavin. Jim was walking alongside him threatening to walk off and leave him if he was sick.

'It'll be me has to get you up into bed as always,' Jim tugged at Gavin's arm. Then he turned to me, 'He's fallen down them ruddy stairs more times than he's walked up 'em.'

In front of us were Sal and Colin. He was talking and she was skipping slightly ahead, her big boots carrying out ballet-steps into the street. I was thinking about the end of Summer, and thinking maybe it would still be too soon to start looking for a job.

As it's such a steep hill, there was no way the bus could have stopped, no way that a big, red double-decker could have done anything other than plough through him and crush his body underneath. There seemed to be noise from everywhere, screeching of tyres, screams from all around, thuds and bangs. And then complete silence. Stillness and silence.

Sal had already reached the other side of the road. Her large, unlaced boots had clomp-skipped her there and she turned round to face us from the opposite kerb at the moment Colin was struck by the bus. She was standing, open-mouthed, frozen in the moment of horror.

My theory is he'd been looking at her arse as she skipped across the road. I remember exactly what she was wearing, that dark green dress which stopped about six inches above the knee. He was always checking her out and I don't think he could take his eyes off her backside as she headed across the road.

Only, this time he'd been found out, by a great big

red double-decker bus.

    I didn't want to go to the funeral. If you hate someone's guts it doesn't seem right. But the others said we should go. It was a much bigger affair than I thought it would be. How the hell did he know so many people? I bet they were all like me, feeling uncomfortable in a suit and tie, looking forward to getting the fuck out of there.

    His mum was back from France with her ridiculously young husband. And he was holding on to her while she cried and swayed about like she and her son had been close or something. And there were loads of Colin's workmates, the men with those stupid fucking haircuts with the fin down the centre, the women with their orange faces. Self-obsessed and vacuous, every one of them.

    All the pews were full. So Jim and Gavin were standing at the back of the church looking like a skinny version of the Blues Brothers, minus the shades. And Sal was standing alone a few paces away from them wearing a black trouser suit that didn't suit her.

    I was standing down the side of the church next to a couple of aunt-like creatures who smelt of biscuits and lavender and sang the hymns really loud. So I could see the others, but I didn't talk to any of them until afterwards when I caught up with them as we entered the pub.

    We met Colin's mum and her French beau on the way in, shaking hands in a line-up like you do at a wedding, everyone saying something like 'I'm sorry for your loss', when they're not, they're actually dying for a fucking sausage roll and a gin and tonic. Thankfully, we got through it and over to the bar in pretty quick time. I bought a round of drinks. Jim spotted a table.

    Sal said we should go over to the buffet and get ourselves some sandwiches while there was still plenty left.

It was a decent spread, pasta and rice dishes, and salads and cooked meats. We took our heaped-high plates back to our seats. And we sat.

Gavin raised his glass.

'To Colin,' he said.

'Colin,' said Sal raising hers.

The four of us touched glasses and each took a sip of drink. And I was thinking 'Thank fuck that's over.'

I couldn't finish all the food.

'I'm going outside for a fag,' I said, 'Anyone want to join me?'

No one did. I took a look over at Sal, flashed her a quick smile. This must have been a rough day for her after what she'd been through that night.

I stood at the back of the beer garden on the little patio where they sometimes had barbeques. There weren't many people around, just a few couples at one or two of the picnic tables. I puffed away at my cigarette and took the opportunity to think about what I should do with my life. The first thing of course was to get a job. Nothing serious, just a way of earning money, serving in a shop somewhere like I did at Dad's. Then I could tap the parents for a loan so I could get set up on my own selling something or other online. Not sure what, but that's where the money is, isn't it? Dad would only lend me the money if he saw me making something of my life, being at least a little independent.

That's when I had the idea. And I wasn't sure why I hadn't thought of it before. It seemed so obvious. Mum had mentioned it a couple of times recently. 'It's not right,' she said, 'someone of your age living with their parents.' I thought she was being a selfish cow at the time, that she just wanted the extra space in the lounge and in her fridge, but now I realised she had a point.

We should all get a place together. It made perfect sense. Jim and Gavin had just been moaning about how much the rents were in London. And Sal hated her creepy landlord and her pokey little flat. It would be cheaper if we rented together, the four of us. I dropped my cigarette to the patio floor and stubbed it out beneath my shoe. I picked up my pint glass and headed back indoors.

It was still busy inside, Colin's family and friends were talking and eating and drinking, most of them choosing to stand despite there being plenty of chairs available. I made my way through, squeezing between conversations, flashing the odd fake smile. But when I got to our table all I found were three half-empty glasses and four empty chairs. I guessed they must have gone to look for me, presuming I was smoking out the front at the side of the street.

I drunk up the last of my pint and went off to find them and tell them my great new idea.

COURT IN A TRAP

Judge speaks.

How do you plead?
Not guilty?
On what grounds?
Lack of free will.
Is this a joke?
I cannot say.
Did you kill your wife?
She died as a result of actions assigned to me.
By whom?
That's the question I'd like answered.
I'm sorry?
It's hardly your fault.
I shall hold you in contempt.
You know, I've literally no idea what will happen next.

There is a loud bang as the court doors open.
The man's wife enters, very much alive.

Crikey. I wasn't expecting that.

ONE WEDNESDAY

John and Marjory liked to have sex on a Wednesday. There was no episode of Eastenders to miss, and Sarah, their cleaner, always changed the bed linen on a Tuesday. John wouldn't eat garlic until Thursday. Marjory would turn off her phone so her mother couldn't call.

This particular Wednesday was a cool, Summer's evening at the end of June. John came home early as always, leaving the office at four on the dot. He opened the door and called out.

'Marj, I'm home.'

There was no reply.

He took off his shiny, brogue work-shoes and placed them neatly in the shelving unit by the front door. He made his way up the stairs expecting to find his wife in the bedroom waiting for him. But, when he stepped inside, she wasn't there.

John opened the wardrobe. Her red, silk negligee was still hanging up inside.

'But it's Wednesday,' John said out loud to the empty room.

He closed the wardrobe door and went to the open bedroom door that faced the landing.

'Marj,' he called. 'It's Wednesday.'

His voice left the bedroom door, and echoed down the stairs, and through the empty house. He walked thoughtfully from the doorway and sat on the edge of the bed with no idea what to do. He looked at the wardrobe door behind which the red, silk negligee was hanging.

Marjory wasn't wearing any underwear. A light breeze flowed up her skirt as she waited for Tom to arrive. When he had suggested they meet on a Wednesday, she had at first felt troubled, and later, rather thrilled. She saw him arriving. She watched as the waiter showed him to their table where she was already seated.

She tried to look cool. She was burning hot.

Tom arrived by her side. He leaned in and kissed her on the cheek.

'At last,' he said, 'I have you to myself.'

He wasn't handsome. But he was clever, and extremely funny. And he wanted her. Over the last six months, he had made that very clear every time they made coffee together in the staff room, or when they arrived in the car park at the same time each day, parking next to each other in the shade of the trees.

They ate mussels in a garlic sauce. Marjory told Tom about her love of gardening. He told her about his passion for collecting old coins. Their legs brushed together. Marjory felt the breeze battling against the heat of her body. They finished with creme brulee. And Tom told her again.

'I am so happy you said yes, that it's just you and me for once.'

'Me too,' She touched his hand, 'I've wanted this for a long time.'

Tom delicately placed his other hand on top of Marjory's.

'Let's not let the evening end here. Is it too much to ask you to come back to mine?'

Marjory looked at their hands entwined, and then to the watch on her wrist. It was thirty-four minutes past ten.

'Let's go for a walk first,' she said.

John called all of Marjory's friends, starting with Gillian at number forty-one. As a last resort, he even called her mother. But no-one knew where she was. He had sent three text messages reminding her it was Wednesday. He looked at the bedside alarm clock. It was three minutes past eleven; too late now.
He went downstairs to turn on the dishwasher before brushing his teeth and going to bed.

As they walked through the park, their path dimly lit by nearby streetlights, Marjory found she couldn't stop talking.
'We used to go to Camber Sands every Summer when I was little. Those were the happiest of days…'
And…
'When we were just 17, Louise and I, that's my cousin, Edith's eldest, we missed the last bus and ended up sleeping on the beach…'
And…
'I love the sound of birdsong. It filters everything else out, until only you and the Earth exist…'
Tom pointed across the road.
'My house is just over there, last one on the right.'
She took his arm and they walked slowly. Marjory looked up at the church clock tower. It was eleven twenty-seven.

John was a little concerned. But he had work in the morning. He took a sleeping tablet, as always. The time on the alarm clock read eleven thirty-nine. He picked up his phone and texted Marjory one last time: 'Gone to bed. Dishwasher on'.

Marjory sat on the sofa next to Tom. He leaned over to kiss her. She made sure she aimed her lips at his this time, not her cheek. She held him tightly in both arms. Inside, she was fiery hot. As their lips and tongues intertwined, she opened one eye. Behind Tom was a carriage clock on the mantelpiece. The time was eleven fifty-three.

She stood up and took Tom's arm, leading him towards the bedroom. Five minutes later they were both naked in the half-light. Tom was lying on the bed. Marjory was standing, looking down at him. Slowly she removed her wristwatch. She lay it on Tom's chest as she climbed across him. She watched the last few seconds tick by.

'It's Thursday,' she said, as she lowered herself down and Tom was inside her.

LEAVING

I am thinking
    Thinking about the line that runs across my face, one of many which were never there in my youth. This one runs across the ridge of my nose forming a groove in which to place spectacles. The line appeared in the mirror the day after I lost my mother. The day after a massive heart attack brought an end to her massive personality. I first saw the line – or wrinkle, if you like – in the lift as I left the hospital. A young face then, with a solitary crack across its youthful sheen; a crack that indicated the increasingly hasty passing of time.

I am looking down
    Down at the people peopling below, as I see them as they really should be seen: miniscule due to the distance between us. I am thinking of my mother and all that she was. She was taken away in a second, removed from this Earth as swiftly and as easily as a bug beneath a boot.
    My face is all lines and wrinkles now. My once smooth skin is segmented by cracks and furrows, each section a reminder of moments on life's journey – not a trip I would recommend.
    The bags which droop beneath my eyes like hippos in hammocks came to stay after Tom left. I always expected him to go of course; even encouraged it. After the children had gone he had no reason to stay. I was a bucket for sperm, an incubator of offspring, and a maker of nests. The bags were a stamp of disapproval. I may as well have been branded with the words 'past its use-by date.'

At least three of my chins arrived when Jake moved away. I am well aware that "it's only a few hours on an aeroplane", but he has still gone. I cannot feel him near me. I have done all I can as far as he is concerned. I popped him out of a hole far too small and brought him into a world which is too large for us to be together.

With a son in Italy, a mother in the afterlife and an ex-husband in court, my hair was bound to turn grey. My crow's feet began to resemble dinosaur footprints and my eyelids receded into their sockets as if to drag my eyes away from what was left to be seen.

Now Katie will soon be gone. I can't be the mother I want to be. I can't tell her the things she needs to hear. I can't take away the pain. She's only thirty-three with a face as smooth as mine once was. Even with a shaved head, she is beautiful. She should be staying around. Bless my beautiful daughter, with a mother like me.

My cheek bones disappeared on May the 13th 1987. a blotched and cracked terrain appeared in their place right in the middle of a party. There was champagne and I was surrounded by good people gathered to celebrate my retirement. They were all smiles and jealousy whilst I stood at the centre of the room knowing that I was but a few hours from leaving behind the last supporting column holding up my very existence.

May's face is always cheerful, hopeful, radiant. She is older than me of course but she shines like the sun – the rest of us making up her solar system, revolving, around her at a respectful distance. But then no-one ever left May. No-one ever wanted to.

I never had a day off work due to stress or illness. Cancer is cruel enough to have bypassed me on its way to one of my children. But greater than stress, depression or insanity, more harmful than high blood pressure, angina, or the mighty cancer, greater than all of these is loneliness. This is the true epidemic sweeping the world. No-one lives in family-units any more. No-one speaks to their neighbours over the garden fence.

Leaving is now a part of the human life cycle: After you leave the home of your childhood, an adulthood of leaving and being left lies ahead of you.

I am crying

Just a solitary tear which is making its break for freedom. It is making its journey over hill and down dale, and it is dripping from my chin, slowly, taking pleasure in making its choice to slip down and down to the ground below.

I am thinking

Thinking of swimming lessons at Junior school. I am remembering how I used to jump into the pool. I can see the different ways of jumping in: bomb, straddle-jump, jack-knife. Then I can see me diving at the age of ten straight arms and legs as you enter the water.

I wonder if the tear has reached the floor yet.

I am jumping

With straight arms and legs, feet first, jack-knife style. I am sinking down to the street below.

This time, I am leaving.

TRENCH WARFARE

It's not the fear that does you in. It's the boredom.

There was plenty of fighting in the trenches. Not with the Boche, but between ourselves. The captain tried to keep us busy, mending sections of wall and pulling broken rotting duckboards from the mud. But in the end the mud seeped through and into everything. And the boredom seeped through just the same.

It simply isn't normal, all those men thrown together in the cold and the rain and the mud. I suppose that's why we'd pick a fight about the slightest thing. Normal rules simply don't apply when you're at war.

Jimmy Foster was a big brute, broad-shouldered and menacing looking. Back at the Two Feathers, even after a few pints of ale, I would never have picked a fight with him. But in the trenches there was nothing to do except wait, and think, and lose your mind over the smallest thing.

It was all over a postcard, a bit dog-eared, of a beautiful landscape. I don't know where it was, somewhere with mountains. The sky was clear above a valley where half a dozen houses nestled together.

I found it in a café. So it was mine.

I used to look at it when I was feeling low. After the war this was where I'd go – somewhere calm, somewhere peaceful, where the people wished each other good morning and quietly went about their business.

I was upset when it went missing. Everywhere I went I looked down at the soggy ground hoping to see it laying there. And then I saw Foster with it, sitting on a sandbag, smoking a fag, escaping into my dream world.

'Bastard.' that's what I called him. Even among the men I wasn't one for cursing. But I can't deny that's what I said.

I gave him a chance to give it back. But he replied with some choice words of his own. Then I was on him, punching him in the chest.

He threw both arms around me. Lowering one shoulder, he easily managed to throw me to the floor. But I kept punching. And calling out 'bastard.'

I could hear voices all around as the others came to watch and laugh and cheer us on. I remember Chipper Colstone shouting 'Easton's lost his marbles.' And Billy Mckintey, who did like to swear, saying 'Fuck me, it's David versus Goliath without the slingshot.'

We rolled in the mud throwing punch after punch and insult after insult. Until the Captain turned up and half a dozen men pulled us apart.

As I was lifted up, I managed to reach down to the ground. I picked up the postcard which had fallen there. It was browned now by the Earth. But it was mine again. I shoved it into my pocket.

Captain Lyons was busy writing a letter when we went to see him. Probably to his parents. I don't think he had a family. Not one he ever spoke of. He hardly looked up. Wanted to write his letter in peace, I guess.

'Is it not enough that we have the Hun to worry about without fighting between ourselves?'

We didn't answer, just stood, our caps in our hands, waiting. Then the Captain did look up. He looked tired. We all did.

'Thankfully you'll be too busy to worry about your petty squabble after today. I suggest you avoid each other tonight and concentrate on getting a good night's sleep. Big day tomorrow.'

And that was it.

I was right by the ladder, which meant I should be able to get over the top nice and quick. I probably wouldn't get picked off in the crush.

And then that bloody whistle.

And we were over.

Nothing appeared to happen at first. I just walked. The world seemed brighter and for a few seconds I thought I might just walk straight forwards right out of this war. Then I began to hear the screams, and explosions. I stumbled on, head down, avoiding looking ahead. Men brushed by me and pieces of earth and heaven only knows what splattered my body from all sides.

Beside me I saw a few faces that I knew, travelling grimly forwards. I spotted Colstone looking at me from the side. He tripped, falling to his knees, rose again and continued onwards. And I saw Willy Harris looking up at the sky, screaming words I couldn't understand. And around us countless other faceless men shouted and wailed and fell and got blown apart or punctured or shredded.

Then I reached a trench – long-abandoned – one of ours or one of theirs I couldn't tell, and I clambered down. There were men crouching inside mustering the courage from somewhere to go out again and face the stream of bullets and shells and thunder.

One by one they climbed out and continued on towards the enemy's lines. Intent on doing their duty. But not all. Three remained. And for the first time I saw that there were dead men in the trench. One body was just a few feet away. A large broad-shouldered man flat on his back.

Barely recognisable, Foster lay breathing heavily, his eyes staring at me as though he'd forgotten how to blink.

His lower jaw had been blown away and his chest was open on one side, which was now a mass of blood and guts and pieces of his uniform.

I made my way towards him on all fours. Shouts and screams from above seemed to become more distant. Occasional showers of earth rained down on us.

He was already dead and we both knew it. If he'd been able to talk it would have made no difference. There was nothing to say. So I held his hand. I lay down next to him and held his hand.

I could hear his breathing, the blood gurgling in his throat, choking him, flooding him. Smoke drifted through the air and the once-deafening explosions seemed dull and distant. Foster gave a last squeeze of my hand and then a raspy, liquidy exhale.

I thought of home, of the Two Feathers.

I was covered from head to toe in dark sticky mud. And drenched down one side in Foster's blood. I got to my knees, put my hands to his disfigured face, and slowly closed his eyes. I pulled the postcard from my pocket. It was a little redder now, to go with the brown, but the picturesque valley was still clearly visible. I slipped the postcard into Foster's hand. I closed my own eyes and said a prayer to a God I had stopped believing in long ago.

Then I climbed into the unknown, leaving Foster to the worms.

There were bodies everywhere and smoke drifted across the scorched and damaged land. I had no idea whether I was heading back towards our lines or forwards or sideways when I fell down and down.

They told me later it was Captain Lyons dragged me under the tree. He must have thought I was badly injured being covered in so much blood.

I drifted in and out of consciousness.
Eventually night fell and the screams almost stopped.

SOMETHING HAD TO BE DONE

No-one can quite work out how Frank has managed to get the branch stuck in his arse-hole.

Ever since he came to them, as a doe-eyed rescue puppy, he has loved leaping around in the undergrowth, never happier than when walking in the woods, straying far from his owners. But this has never happened before.

If it were possible for a rottweiler to purse his lips, this is exactly how you would describe the look on Frank's face.

Something had to be done.

'You need to get TWO fingers up there.' Elliott says.

Melissa's eyes are closed. She misses her target like a disorientated child trying to pin a tail on a donkey. She gives up, pulls her hand away and opens her eyes. She looks at Elliott who's standing some distance away looking pained, as if he is the one with a branch stuck in his arse-hole.

'Isn't there something about loosening a dog's arse by sticking your fingers in its mouth.'

'I think it's the other way around.' Says Elliott.

The offending branch is about a foot long. Judging by the secure nature of its positioning, at least two inches of it is wedged inside Frank.

'Come over and hold him,' says Melissa, 'He looks petrified.'

Elliott inches towards his best friend in the world.

He holds out his hands to Frank as he slowly approaches.

'It's ok mate, we'll sort it out.'

Rain starts to fall, little patters, then a gushing downpour. As a result, Melissa springs into action, as though things have somehow become more urgent.

'Right, you hold him, as tight as you can around his neck, and I'll pull the branch.'

Elliott puts his arms around Frank.

'Here we go Buddy,' he says, 'Soon be over.'

But Melissa stops. 'Hang on,' she says.

She reaches into her handbag and pulls out a silver-blue, disc-shaped pot. She flips off the lid and uses two fingers to scope out a huge glob of lip balm. She sets about smearing it around Frank's sphincter, her fingers circling gently.

Frank barks. It's not clear whether the lip balm has improved things for the dog or whether this is a bark of distress.

Melissa clasps the stick tightly. Elliott hugs Frank. On the count of three, they both pull. Frank howls instantly and they stop. The branch stays put.

Melissa is on the phone now. To her mother.

'It's a silver birch, I think.' She pauses. "Is that important?"

Elliott looks over at her curiously. But before he can speak he is distracted by movement.

They both look towards the dog who is surely, but very slowly, on the move Frank is panting, shuffling into the undergrowth. There, he crouches. Painfully he pushes. The branch begins to edge its way out. At its end, the dog end, it is followed by a large turd. Eventually the stick falls to the ground, pushed entirely out of the arse-hole by a solid black-brown dog-shit.

Frank runs off to play in the woods.

THE PIPS ON RADIO 4

'I'll miss you.'

Talking to the radio is not something I usually do. But the reassuring sound of the Archer's theme tune, the Shipping Forecast, the pips before the news - the radio really will be one of the things I'll miss when I'm dead and gone. And I've never been good at talking to people so I suppose it makes sense that I should be opening up to the gadget in the kitchen.

I realise I've been there for some time, leaning against the work surface, staring out the French windows at nothing in particular. Woman's hour has begun. Emma Barnett is talking to a woman about her relationship with her mother. I don't know who she is – or who her mother is – but the radio is soothing, as much as anything can be today.

But I have to leave Emma and the woman behind. I have to collect the washing from the kid's rooms. It's one of the jobs that needs to be done, that will fill the time before we leave, one of the jobs I've planned to fill the void.

Tom's room is, as always, difficult to negotiate. Clothes and books and discarded Amazon packaging litter the floor. But, to his credit, he has made the bed as I asked. I pick up a t-shirt from behind the door and I can't avoid smelling it. Like all teenage boys, there is a musty, unwashed odour.

But the smell is also unique to Tom. How would I

describe it? A mixture of crushed biscuits, soil, and lavender. I plunge my nose into the t-shirt and fill my lungs with the smell. I am thinking of all the parents who have lost a child, who will never smell them again. My heart is heavy. I shall miss this smell when I am dead and gone. I shall miss Tom.

Izzy's room is next, a little more ordered. She's not hit the teenage years yet, but there are signs. Dolls sit on a top shelf gathering dust and her bedside table has been taken over by garish trinkets, a collection of friendship bracelets, and a pink Bluetooth speaker. I haven't been in this room for a week and there's a new addition, a photo-collage on the wall, pictures of Izzy and her friends laughing and smiling, making rabbit ears behind each other's heads. These days we share more arguments than hugs, but there she is, my little girl, and she's happy. She's growing up, making friends, finding out who she is. One day she'll leave here a grown-up and never look back. From the day she was born I wanted to protect her, make the world safe for her. And I'll miss her when I'm dead and gone.

I push these morbid thoughts out of my mind. I must not think about the end. I've been prone to doing that lately. I've never been one to dwell, never been one to analyse. The clock is ticking and there are several jobs to be done before we leave. 'Keep busy', I tell myself, 'Fill the void'.

I place the laundry basket in the hall and head for our bedroom. As I pass the bathroom, I can hear the shower running. And I can hear the singing that usually makes me smile. Today it only increases the pain in feel in my chest.

I'll keep busy. Not much time and plenty of jobs to do.

The curtains are still closed in our room. I open them and one of the windows. For a moment I lean on the sill and look out at the garden, thinking again of what I shall miss when I am dead. The apple tree we planted the first year in the house is ripe with fruit. The shed we built together needs painting or knocking down. A wasp flies in through the window. I flap about until it makes its way back through the open window to the outside world. The disturbance has stopped me dreaming. I remember there are jobs to be done.

I promised I would strip the bed and turn the mattress. We were told to do this when we bought it. We haven't yet done it once. It's a job that needs doing. And I need to keep busy.

When the sheets and pillowcases are off, I struggle to flip the mattress over. It falls down with a thud and the subsequent gust of air brushes bits of paper from the bedside table. I pick them up and tut, not that anyone is around to hear. There are bank statements, flyers for take-away pizza and empty envelopes all mixed together, opened, briefly read and then discarded. They haven't come from my side of the bed. I never do this. 'Always deal with post as it arrives, otherwise the place will be covered in papers before you know it.' I've said it a hundred times. No-one in the family listens. Like most families, I guess they never will.

I throw the bedclothes through the doorway into the hall to join the kids' laundry. I sort the papers into two piles, one of things to keep and the other of things to throw away. I take the latter pile with me into the hall and place it on top of the washing in the basket.

From the bathroom I can feel the steamy heat slipping beneath the door. I am just about to take the basket downstairs when there is a sound, a clunk, as something hits the floor, and the sound of the shower stops. I hear more thumping sounds, and then the sound of wet feet coming out of the shower. Clumsily.

I move towards the bathroom door.

'You ok?'

There is no answer. I knock.

'Everything alright?'

Then Jane opens the door, surrounded by steam. She stands in the doorway dripping, smiling.

Jane has always loved the shower. She can spend hours in there. She calls it her 'karaoke booth'. Seeing her emerge, singing, jiggling her hips, with one towel wrapped around her body and another stacked up to conceal her long hair, I know I've married the right woman.

She doesn't need the second towel any more of course. She no longer has her long hair.

'I heard a noise, thought you might have fallen.'

She leans over, holding her towel about her with one hand, touching my arm with the other. And she kisses me on the forehead.

'I'm fine,' she says, 'Dropped the shower-head that's all. Did you say you were making tea?'

I didn't of course.

'Will you be ok?'

She looks at me. And the look is enough to tell me the answer: 'Stop worrying, relax, make tea.'

She comes down dressed but still sodden.

'You're not properly dry. You'll catch your death,' I say.

'It's not cold,' she replies, 'I'm fine.'

I pass her a mug of tea.

'How was Tom's room?'

'You know...aromatic.'

We take our tea to the kitchen table and sit together

as we have done so many times before. There's a drama on the radio now, something set during the war about a pilot who never returns from a mission. It's being told from the point of view of his wife, or maybe his girlfriend, maybe even his mistress. We sit without talking, half listening to the story, drinking our tea. The woman telling the story is old now, looking back in later life at the love she lost.

My chair is a bit wobbly. I probably should be listening to the woman —she's getting quite emotional — but I'm wondering whether there is time for me to get a screwdriver and tighten up the chair-legs.

'We should be going soon,' Jane says, 'The traffic can be appalling on Church Street.'

'I just have to fill in that form for Izzy, you know, the museum trip. And write a cheque. Don't want to forget.'

She knows I am stalling. And she says nothing.

Jane is putting her shoes on, which takes a long time. I fetch our coats from the cupboard. I know she won't let me help with the shoes.

'Have you got the folder?' she calls.

I hate the folder.

'It's on the table,' I say.

In fact, we have two folders. One is blue and it contains all the doctors' notes, hospital appointments and advice leaflets from the last eighteen months. The other is yellow and contains all the information given to us by the Hospice. It's the yellow one she means because there's no point in the other one anymore.

Jane has her shoes on. She has picked up the yellow folder and joins me in the hall. I help her on with her coat, a gentlemanly act, not patronising assistance. And it's time to go.

I'm frozen to the spot. After all this time, all that

we've been through, this is a decision I have to make and one I don't want to – to take Jane to visit the place where she has chosen to die. To make arrangements. And that in itself is ridiculous. She hasn't 'chosen' anything. 'We' haven't chosen anything.

It's not me that's dying, but I too am losing everything. I'm not the one in pain, though. And I've wondered about that thing that you hear people say: Would I change places with her if I could? I don't know. I only know I don't want it to be her *or* me. I don't want it to happen to *us*.

She takes me by the arm. I think I should say something, something touching, or at least something normal to put her at her ease. But nothing comes. I'm not good with words.

'Come on, we don't want to be late,' she says.

I don't want to go at all.

We've left the house and I've checked three times that I've locked the door. We have the yellow folder and the sat nav knows where to go. The engine is running and radio 4 is on.

Glenn Miller's In the Mood is playing. The woman has finished telling the story of the pilot. And I'm frozen again. My hands are on the wheel and I'm staring at nothing in particular.

The pips begin. It is eleven o'clock. Time for the news on radio 4. And time for us to leave.

I'm crying. Big sobs. I haven't cried in years. Jane reaches out and touches my left hand on the wheel. I turn to look at her. I want her to stay.

There is so little time and so much to say, but I've never been good at talking. So I say the only words that will come, the only words I know to be true.

'I'll miss you.'

PAST, PRESENT, AND FUTURE

He only wanted a pint of milk. But he could see them waiting, hooded and hunched, leaning against the wall where they could be found for most of the day. Six youths – probably aged about fifteen or so – laughing, smoking, pushing one another around.

George had never had time in his life just to 'hang around'. He recalled his sixteenth birthday and the pride he felt when his signature had been accepted at the recruitment office. He remembered his mother's face as he returned with the news. She'd looked at her youngest son with pride, whilst he knew she felt a mother's fear.

By seventeen he'd watched men die, seen the fear of death. And it had made him want to live. For two long years he'd struggled each night to sleep, as the world around him seemed full of explosions, and the nightmares in his head were even more dreadful than the reality to which he awoke. By his eighteenth birthday he had returned home to a mother who seemed to have aged incredibly.

Now he was looking through the smallest of gaps between the net-curtains at a group of young men with nowhere to go and nothing to do. And it would take all the courage he had just to pass them standing there, so that he could go to the shop for a pint of milk.

When had he become so fearful?

When had his mind and body become those of an old man?

Michael pulled his hood down over his forehead as the cold wind that rushed between the tower-blocks hit him hard. He was bored. He'd spent so many hours leaning against the same wall, listening to Ricky drone on about the latest tunes or the fittest girl at school.

He was thinking about what Mr Brown had said:

'If you put your mind to it, you could get a B in your English, maybe even an A if you're willing to do the extra work.'

No-one at his school had ever expected anything of him before. He was just another kid from the estate. They expected him to get into trouble, expected him not to care, even expected him to stop turning up at all. But that wasn't what he felt inside. He was going to make something of himself. He would show Mr Brown he was right. And he would make his mother proud.

He knew his mother had done everything she could for him. He knew she hated her job, hated the estate, and hated being single. It had all been for him, the relentless hours at the supermarket, the jumble-sale cardigans she wore, and the holidays she had never taken.

But he still felt like a kid, her kid. He wanted to prove to her that everything she had worked for had been worthwhile. Then maybe she would leave the estate one day. Maybe she would travel the world.

But he was just a kid, with dreams and anger in equal measure. Where could he find the strength to succeed? Ricky and the others seemed perfectly happy hanging around in the street, talking about girls and nodding to music that only they could hear.

He could see the old man staring at them from behind his net-curtains, no doubt thinking of calling the police, thinking they were up to no good. This pissed

Michael off more than anything. He couldn't help being fifteen. He couldn't help having been born into this shit-hole. He couldn't help the fact that he had nothing better to do. Not yet anyway.

George put his coat on. Maybe they would go home soon; even hoodies must have mothers who would have dinner ready for them occasionally. He was furious with himself for waiting.

Why should an old man be afraid to step out of his own front door? Jean would have pushed him outside. But Jean wasn't there. He would have given anything to have just five minutes with her again, to listen to her talking about Margaret's new carpet, or describing what she loved about Rhododendrons, even to hear her whispered voice during those last painful days when they had laughed and cried and said goodbye.

Yes. She would have laughed at him, kissed him on the cheek and opened the front door.

Michael looked at the old man's face peering from behind the net-curtains. And he knew he didn't want to end up like that, living alone in this sad place, having done nothing with his life.

George closed the curtains. He walked to the door and stood with his eyes closed, one hand on the door handle. He let Jean's image come into his head and imagined her kissing his cheek. He opened the door and strode purposefully out. He wanted a pint of milk.

Michael watched as the door opened and the old man stepped outside.

'Look out, Granddad,' shouted Ricky, 'There's some

nasty folk about.'

Michael thought Ricky was a prat. He could see the old man was scared.

'For God's sake Ricky,' he said, 'Just for once, why don't you shut up.'

George continued on his way to the shop. He passed the group of youths. He didn't look over in their direction.

Michael walked away from Ricky and the others. He removed his hood and ran his fingers through his hair. His footsteps were young and quick. It wasn't long before he was overtaking George. He glanced across at the wrinkled face with its glassy eyes. 'I'm never ending up like that,' he thought.

George watched the young man speed by with his hands in his pockets, his shoulders drooping forwards. 'I was never like that,' he thought.

It was then that George slipped, falling onto his side with his left leg tucked underneath him. Instinctively Michael turned to help him up.

'You alright old man?'

'Old man?' thought George, 'A stupid, old man.'

Holding on to Michael's outstretched arms, he got to his feet. His left knee was so painful that he simply gritted his teeth and failed to respond.

'Let's get you inside,' said Michael. He gestured to the café just a few yards away, standing next to the shop where George was going to buy a pint of milk.

Michael brought two mugs of tea over to the table. The old man looked up at him, the shock of the fall beginning to disappear from his face.

'I'm Michael.'

'George,' said the old man reaching out a cold, wrinkled hand to shake the warm, smooth-skinned hand belonging to Michael.

'Not staying with your friends then?' George asked.

'No,' answered Michael.

George pointed at the sugar bowl on the table just out of his reach. Michael slid it along the table towards him.

'Thanks,' said George adding three spoonfuls to his tea.

'No problem old man.'

'Less of the 'old',' replied George with a smile. He lifted his tea to his mouth and blew across the surface to cool it down.

'I've seen you,' said Michael, 'Watching us through the curtains.'

'And I've seen you,' said George, 'hanging around.'

'What's your plan old man? Where were you going today?'

'I just need a pint of milk.' He said.

'Must be quite a chore, You know, walking at that pace.'

George laughed.

'I bet old-age seems so very far away to you.' He sipped his tea noisily, 'And you? Not hanging around with the hoodies?'

It was Michael's turn to laugh.

'Who the hell still uses the word 'hoodie'?' he said.

'Who the hell goes around calling people old?'

George sat back in his chair. He stared out of the window.

'It doesn't look very interesting loitering in the street day after day,' he said, 'And I don't think your friend was very impressed with you telling him to shut up.'

'That's the first time I've ever stood up to Ricky,' said Michael, 'Not so much a daring thing to do. More of a bloody stupid thing.'

'So you were finally standing up for yourself. And you helped me out. I guess I should thank you.'

'Maybe,' mumbled Michael, 'I can't stand it here any longer. Nothing changes. I see the same faces, talk about the same things.'

George took a gulp of tea and then looked up at Michael.

'What are you going to do then?' he asked.

'You really want to know?'

'Of course I do.'

'I'm hoping to become a teacher,' This was the first time he had stated it aloud.

'Good for you young man.'

'Thanks old man.'

George smiled. Michael smiled too.

'The problem is…'

'Yes?'

'The problem is, it takes guts, doesn't it? I have to stop coming out each night to see the others. They won't understand. Maybe it's easier to forget about it.'

'My wife died seventeen years ago today.'

'Sorry?'

'My wife,' continued George, 'I watched her slowly fade away.'

'Why are you telling me?'

'Because,' said George calmly, 'I needed a pint of milk. And I didn't even dare leave my own home.' He winked at Michael, 'Hoodies everywhere.'

Michael drank his tea. George looked out of the window again. Then he turned back to the young man.

'Tell you what,' said George, 'I dare you to go back

now and tell them.'

'You dare me?'

'Yep,' said George, 'Just walk up to that big fella. Ricky is it? And tell them: I'm going to make something of myself.'

Michael looked away.

'Ok, but on one condition,' He said, turning back to face George, 'I dare you to come with me.'

George was eighty-one years old. He'd already lived a long life. If it ended now at the hands of some hoodie then at least he could see Jean sooner than he thought.

'Ok,' he said. 'But we'll have to pop next door first. I need a pint of milk.'

SECURE IN THE KNOWLEDGE THAT EVERYTHING HAPPENS FOR A REASON

This time he had a chance. He might actually win something. But the taxi was coming at 7.30. And it didn't look like Clive was going to be ready. Because Clive had stapled three sheets of paper to his left hand.

He hadn't meant to of course but then how many people do intentionally staple anything at all to any part of their body?

He was wondering whether it would be extremely painful if he were to try to remove the staple.

It wasn't just hanging on the surface layer of skin; He'd pushed down hard on the table, not realising the flap between his thumb and first finger was between the piece of paper and the hard surface. So it was well and truly attached.

And it ached. But the act of removing it would mean ripping the flesh. The little metal clasp had closed in on itself and secured itself extremely, well, securely.

He waved his hand slowly through the air. The paper flapped about. It wasn't so bad, he thought. His movements were hardly restricted at all.

Whenever there was a stabbing, or impaling in a hospital drama on telly, the paramedics always advised against removing the offending article for fear of making things worse. Clive became concerned that if he were to remove the staple a fountain of blood would ensue and, rather than be left with a slightly encumbered left hand and a dull, mildly irritating ache, he would start to lose blood, fast. An image popped into his mind, an image of Sonia, his cleaner on her weekly visit discovering him lying on the conservatory floor, as white as a sheet, drained of blood.

So, for now, he wasn't going to remove the staple. It seemed far too risky and far too painful. It was best left as it was. That would give him time to think. And he was rather hoping it might just dislodge itself and slide off in his sleep. If only he could just conceal it for now.

His thoughts turned to the prize-giving. He might not win of course but not being good at ad-libbing he had thought it best to write something down in advance. Once he'd listed all the people to thank and the advice he had to give to other aspiring screenwriters, the speech had become much longer than he'd anticipated. Three whole pages. Hence the need for a stapler, and the reason why he was now pondering how he would be able to cover up his little mishap before the taxi arrived.

He considered wearing gloves, perhaps just one glove Michael Jackson style. First, he thought it would best to reduce the amount of paper hanging from his hand.

He fetched a pair of scissors from the sideboard and cut the three sheets as close to the staple as he dared. It was a terribly slow process. After the mishap with the stapler, Clive wasn't sure he could be trusted with scissors so close to his own flesh. But eventually, he had trimmed the paper so that all that remained was the staple and a couple of square centimetres of the sheets in a roughly rectangular shape between his finger and thumb - just the right size to cover with a plaster.

He went to the kitchen and pulled open a drawer. Amongst the several million paper-clips, bottle tops, straws and pizza leaflets, he found a plaster which just covered the paper and the offending staple. He also took a paper-clip, returned to the lounge, printed the three sheets of paper out again, and then joined them in a much safer fashion.

It was 7.05.

Using his one good hand, he put his jacket across his shoulders. He looked in the hallway mirror. Maybe this was his time. Just for once.

He checked his pocket for the speech and picked up his keys from the side table. He stepped through the doorway and put his keys in the lock. As always he would make sure he turned the key in all three locks just to be safe.

As the taxi pulled up in the street behind him, he was bathed in light. He turned the key one last time and turned towards the road. As he did so, the key jammed in the lock as he failed to turn it so it was flush with the hole and would come slipping out. His left hand slipped from the keys and he felt a ripping sensation as the key ring lodged first underneath the plaster, and then, after this began to come away, underneath the staple. He couldn't turn around. His momentum was taking him full force away from the door.

The pain was immense as he became separated from the keys and rather more notably from more than a little of his flesh.

He'd landed on the pavement at the bottom of the two steps which led up to his front door. He must have passed out for a short while as the taxi driver was kneeling down next to him and talking on a mobile phone.

"Yes", he said, "Lots of blood. Hang on his eyes are open"

Then Clive noticed the blood which had covered the path around him. He lifted his hands and discovered where the blood had come from. The staple had been removed. Unfortunately, so had a large section of the skin on his left hand.

Clive passed out for the second time.

The night was blighted by the usual stream of overly long, backslapping speeches. A special mention should go to Clive Waterfield who finally broke his duck and won best writer for his play 'Close Attachment'. Sadly, Clive was rushed to hospital shortly before the award ceremony began. We wish him a speedy recovery.

THE TROUBLE WITH MR. GIBSON

<u>Texts across the playground</u>
Charlotte
18 – 10 – 2009 12:45
Have you seen the pictures of Gibbo?

Bethany
18-10 – 2009 12:49
OMG I nearly died laughing. Do you think his wife knows?

Charlotte
18 – 10 – 2009 12:53
If she didn't she soon will. Jake's plastered pictures all over school!!

Bethany
18 – 10 – 2009 12:57
LOL. Serves him right miserable old git

Charlotte
18 – 10 – 2009 13:01
Going to maths then?

Bethany
18 – 10 – 2009 13:05
Wouldn't miss it for the world

<u>Note to all staff</u>
There will be a meeting in the staff room at 4.30pm today. Please arrive promptly.
ALL ARE EXPECTED TO ATTEND

Answer-phone message
Brian? Brian, it's Amanda. Brian?…oh God, when will you learn to answer your bloody phone? We're in trouble. Look, Someone took some photos last night and as you can imagine this makes things rather awkward. Oh God Brian, everyone in the office has seen them. I think you might have problems at work today. I hope to God you check your messages before you leave for work. Call me.

Mr Trimble's speech in assembly
I am sorry to have had to call this assembly as we come up to exam time. I am only too aware that some of you will require all the time you have left in order to gain even the least respectable of marks this Summer.
However, it has been brought to my attention that certain images have been in circulation. I am sure these images will have raised questions in your young minds.
I ask you now to do the sensible thing, not to gossip, but to concentrate on your studies. I will be sending a letter to your parents tomorrow after a meeting later today to discuss matters.
Be under no illusion, children printing images, sending messages of a salacious nature, or those involved in spreading rumours will be dealt with severely.
That is all.

Staff Meeting
MRS BELTCHAM
I never knew he had such lovely legs.

MISS CARTWRIGHT
Quadratic equations by day, leather-clad dancing by night, who'd have thought it?

MR TRIMBLE

Thank you everybody. As we're all here, we might as well begin.

As you know, several photographs which involve a member of staff have caused quite a stir.

I have recommended that our head of Mathematics take the decision to leave with immediate effect.

He has agreed to this request if he is allowed first to talk to you, his colleagues. I have some reservations but…Mr Gibson.

MR GIBSON

Thank you, Headmaster. Colleagues, I must be to the point and I must be honest.

In 2005, my wife and I ran into some financial difficulties. As you know, surviving on a teacher's salary is not easy. It was at this time – when we were close to losing our family home – that my wife, Amanda, met with an old school friend who had just set up a new business in town. He was looking for people of a certain age to come and work for him in the…erm…'entertainment' business. He was offering terribly good money. As members of the Tewksbury Amateur Dramatics Society, both Amanda and I were used to a little…role playing.

We were an instant success in our roles as 'hosts' at the Pink Jaguar club and were soon able to put our money worries behind us.

Unfortunately, the job in question necessitated the wearing of 'unique' work-clothes as well as a little dancing and singing. It is of course a life not usually allied with that of Head of Mathematics at a reputable fee-paying school. Now that it is common knowledge, I am somewhat compromised.

And that's it really. I will of course be resigning immediately.

MISS CARTWRIGHT
He probably makes more money in his other job anyway.

MRS BELTCHAM
God, I would die for a pair of legs like that.

<u>Texts across the playground</u>
Charlotte
19 – 10 – 2009 08:25
Have you heard? Gibbos gone?

Bethany
18-10 – 2009 12:49
No way. Is he coming back?

Charlotte
18 – 10 – 2009 12:53
No. And that woman in the red boots was his wife!!!

Bethany
18 – 10 – 2009 12:57
Nice boots!

Charlotte
18 – 10 – 2009 13:01
Nice wife. How did that happen?

Bethany
18 – 10 – 2009 13:05
LOL. Why has he left? Just cos hes a perv.

Charlotte
19 – 10 – 2009 08:25
I know. He was the best maths teacher I've had.

Bethany
18-10 – 2009 12:49
How we gonna pass GCSE now?

Charlotte
18 – 10 – 2009 12:53
Selfish bastard.

MORNING HAS NOT YET BROKEN

At the end of the garden of his sleepy Surrey home,
The foxes are fucking and he's unable to sleep

The morning will come
He knows it
And the Brompton Bicycles
Will be unfolded smugly
And their lycra-clad owners
Will place them concertinaed
Jagged pedals and handles
Partially blocking the doors

The morning will come
He knows it
And the Phone conversations
Will be wholly one-sided
And the ultra-loud phoners
Will go on never-ending
'He was like, and I was like'
Entirely filling the space.

The foxes are fucking and he's unable to sleep

The morning will come
He knows it

And the armpits and scalps
Will be odorous and flaky
And the pin-striped swayers
Will taste hairspray and bodies
Sweaty foreheads and armpits
Breakfast rising up the throat

The morning will come
He knows it
And the bragging city boys
Will endlessly speak
Of their end-of-the-dayers
When the boys on a mission
Beyond the missionary position
Unfeelingly, fill their time.

The foxes are fucking and he's unable to sleep

And the people he loves
Will not be there
And the hunter/gatherer
Will be battered and bruised
By the not-give-a-shitters
Who bombard him with noises
Ring-tones and drum-beats
Bags and bikes on the floor

He thinks of the cock,
The cock of the fox,
Inserted and doing its business
Barbed and anchored
There is no going back
And the recipient screams
At the end of the garden of his sleepy Surrey home

And the slightly balding man
With whom he has never exchanged a word
Will be there at five past eight
Standing on the same platform
Waiting for the same train
Each morning growing slightly balder

Does he sleep soundly?
Or are there foxes fucking in his garden?

A FINAL WORD

Dearest lovely people,

If you liked **THE FURTHER ADVENTURES OF CLEMENT GOLIGHTLY**, please tell your friends. And keep coming back, as there will be more in the very near future.

Please also look out for **MODERN**, my feature film in development at **SINGULAR FILMS**.

Huge thanks and much love to you all.

Clem

Twitter @mark_clementson

Instagram @clementsonmark

www.singular-films.co.uk

Printed in Great Britain
by Amazon